The Dorset Cream Tea Mystery

Rachel McLean writes bestselling crime and mystery books with characters you'll be rooting for and stories that readers can't put down. Originally a self-publishing sensation, she has sold millions of copies digitally, with massive success in the UK, and a growing reach internationally. She is the author of the Dorset Crime novels and the spin-off McBride & Tanner series and Cumbria Crime series. In 2021, she won the Kindle Storyteller Award with *The Corfe Castle Murders* and her books regularly hit No 1 in the Bookstat ebook chart on launch.

Millie Ravensworth is the pen name of two authors who have been writing entertaining novels together for more than ten years. The Millie Ravensworth books focus on their shared love of crime stories and charming characters who readers love spending time with.

Also by Rachel McLean and Millie Ravensworth

The Lyme Regis Women's Swimming Club series

The Lyme Regis Women's Swimming Club
A Brush with Death

The London Cosy Mysteries series

Death at Westminster
Death in the West End
Death at Tower Bridge
Death on the Thames
Death at St Paul's Cathedral
Death at Abbey Road

The DORSET CREAM TEA MYSTERY

A LYME REGIS WOMEN'S SWIMMING CLUB STORY

RACHEL MCLEAN
MiLLiE RAVENSWORTH

ACKROYD PUBLISHING

Copyright © 2025 by Rachel McLean and Millie Ravensworth

All rights reserved.

No part of this book may be reproduced in any form or by any electronic or mechanical means, including information storage and retrieval systems, without written permission from the author, except for the use of brief quotations in a book review.

This is a work of fiction. Names, characters, businesses, places, events and incidents are either the products of the author's imagination or used in a fictitious manner. Any resemblance to actual persons, living or dead, or actual events is purely coincidental.

Ackroyd Publishing

ackroydpublishing.com

Printed and bound in the UK by CPI Group (Uk) Ltd, Croydon CR0 4YY

Chapter One

Of the many calls Dorset Police received each year from members of the public who'd found a 'dead body', very few turned out to be actual dead bodies.

Most were plastic bags or old boots floating in a secluded pool. Some were scarecrows that had fallen from their perches. Last year, there had been a fly-tipper, still at large, who'd dumped at least twelve clothes shop mannequins in hedges and ditches along the A35 between Bridport and Axminster, prompting a flurry of 999 calls.

But sometimes, it turned out to be a dead body.

In the early morning light, PC Douglas Anderson climbed up the steep bank by the side of Lyme Road, which led down from the main road into Lyme Regis. Reaching the trees at the top of the bank, he saw the dead man on the ground. Todd Collier, who owned Greensleeves Farm, climbed up beside him.

The man was curled up on his side beside the tree roots, as though he was just sleeping. Douglas crouched and put a hand to the man's neck to check for a pulse, but the pale skin, icy to the touch, confirmed what he already knew.

"That's a dead man."

"Told you it was," said Todd.

"Dead body, is it?" called PC Wendy Sharman from the roadside below.

"It is."

Douglas had seen plenty of corpses. It wasn't always crime. When someone died alone at home or was killed in an accident, the police were often the first to attend the scene. And while Douglas had become familiar with the appearance of death, a corpse always brought out his solemn and sympathetic side.

His wife Naomi and his sister-in-law Tina (who was staying with them at the moment) both thought Douglas was a bit of a softie. And that was fine, as far as he was concerned. Having a heart wasn't a bad quality in a copper. He cared about people, in life and in death.

The dead man's hands were held together at his stomach, like he was huddling for warmth. But Douglas could see dried blood on those hands. It looked like he had been clutching a wound as he died.

"Reckon he might have been stabbed or shot," he called down to Wendy.

She climbed up the bank to join him.

Douglas looked around. This was a crime scene now. They'd have to close a section of the road and tape off much of the area.

"Todd," he said to the farmer. "D'you mind going back down to the road?"

"A dead body don't bother me," Todd said.

Douglas pointed to the farmer's boots. "We don't want

any more contamination of the crime scene than we've already got."

"Oh. Right-o, squire."

As Todd backed away, Wendy pointed to items scattered near the man. Coins and banknotes lay on the grass beside a wallet, marked by smeared fingerprints.

"He was going for his phone," she said, pointing it out on the ground just below the man's lifeless fingers.

Douglas nodded. "Think you're right."

He crouched, pulled on a pair of latex gloves and teased open the wallet. Standard procedure was not to disturb anything until CID and CSI got to the scene, but if they could identify the man...

He opened the wallet on the ground, just wide enough to see the driver's licence. Douglas tilted his head to read.

"Anthony Tarone."

"Tarone?" said Wendy.

The name nudged something in Douglas's brain, too. "The Freeman family?"

Wendy sighed. Anthony Tarone was an associate of a known crime group operating out of Exeter and Torquay, further west along the coast. Multiple arrests, plenty of court appearances, and yet the Freeman family crime gang still had their greasy fingers in cocaine distribution across the south west. They were a stain on the region, and notorious enough for two small-town coppers to have heard of one of their trusted lieutenants, Anthony Tarone.

"We don't do gangsters in Lyme," said Wendy.

Douglas turned to her "Today we do."

Chapter Two

Rosamund Winters loved her view over Lyme Regis. Her house was high up, off the Sidmouth Road, and the road dropped away so steeply that nothing impeded her view.

She could perform a weather forecast simply by sitting upright in bed and checking the colour of the sea towards the cliffs at Charmouth. Slate-grey meant rain, but today, cobalt blue promised clear skies and sunshine for her morning swim.

All of which meant she was on the beach early, along with the rest of her little group of friends. The water was still cold in June, but it was exhilarating to swim from the beach to the end of the Cobb, her regular routine. A warming drink at the Kiosk would be the reward.

Annie was the unelected leader of their little group, a woman who laughed easily. Time spent with Annie often ended up in unexpected places.

As Rosamund arrived at the beach, Annie was waiting with Figgy and Helen.

"Today's your first day on the holiday cottage circuit, isn't it, Rosamund?" Annie asked.

"It is!"

Rosamund had spent many years as a homemaker. She'd had a husband, a son and a large house to take care of. Now the husband had left, the son was grown, and the large house needed to be paid for.

She'd just taken on a job cleaning holiday cottages for Hewish Homes, which had something of a monopoly on self-catering accommodation locally.

"Are we still calling it housekeeping rather than cleaning?" asked Helen.

Helen was the artsy bohemian member of the group. Even in her post-swim attire, she looked like a cross between a ballerina and a punk who'd been given ten minutes in a charity shop to assemble an outfit.

"I am calling it that," said Rosamund. "And it's not because I think I'm above cleaning or that I'm a snob."

"Nobody thinks you're a snob," said Figgy.

Figgy was the youngest of their group. She was gaining confidence, but she remained nervous of conflict.

Rosamund smiled at Figgy. "No, of course not. I like the term housekeeper because it feels more like a job I can take pride in. I want to feel that I'm caring for these properties, not just whizzing round with a duster."

"If I know anything about holiday lets," said Annie, "you'll be whizzing round with a bucket of disinfectant and a peg on your nose. I can't wait to hear the horror stories. I'm almost tempted to come and join you, but Tina's going to be in and out with the grandkids. You know how she can't stay away from police work."

Annie's daughter Tina was a detective with the Dorset

Police. She was currently on maternity leave, but the lure of a case was frequently too strong for her to resist.

"Speaking of police," said Helen, "you hear about that business up Lyme Road?"

Rosamund shook her head.

"Police have closed the whole road. Traffic's been diverted down Charmouth Road, which is nose to tail. And apparently a lorry's got stuck following its satnav down St Mary's Lane."

St Mary's Lane was little more than a footpath.

"Ridiculous," said Rosamund.

"I don't drive," said Figgy.

"I've no idea what it's all about," said Helen.

Annie grunted. "Dead body."

The others looked at her. With a daughter and a son-in-law in law enforcement, Annie got more than her share of inside knowledge.

She shrugged. "Our Naomi's Dougie's up there. Tina's been phoning him since the crack of dawn and Naomi can't help but overhear, can she?"

"A dead body," Figgy whispered. Rosamund wasn't sure if the younger woman was shocked or excited.

"Playing bloody havoc with the traffic," said Helen. "Where are you cleaning cottages today, Rosamund?"

"Housekeeping," Rosamund replied automatically. She reached for her notebook. "I start this morning with Clappentail Cottages."

"You planning to drive there?"

She nodded. Her employer had provided her kit, including cleaning products, mops and a hoover. There was no way she could lug all that around by hand.

"I can't believe they started you off with six cottages," said Annie.

"And they don't all have the same changeover dates," said Rosamund. "Short-term lets, a lot of them." She smiled. "I'm hitting the ground running, which is very much the way I like to do things."

Annie tipped her fingers to her head. "Here's to Rosamund hitting the ground running."

"Bloody good luck to you," said Helen. "You'll need it."

Chapter Three

Rosamund had made a list of what needed doing at Clappentail Cottages.

Friday
Cottage 1 – Occupied (Taverner)
Cottage 2 – Unoccupied – Clean – Arrowsmiths arriving today
Cottage 3 – Tyne-Phillips leaving – Clean – Marconis arriving today
Cottage 4 – Occupied (Obeng)
Cottage 5 – Unoccupied – clean tomorrow
Cottage 6 – Fletchers leaving – Clean – Drummonds arriving today

Check-out was at eleven and check-in for the next set of guests was at three. It was ten now, so that gave her an hour for the unoccupied Cottage 2, then four hours for the other two. She could manage that.

But she hadn't reckoned with the traffic. It took fifty minutes to drive the few hundred meters to Clappentail Cottages, by which time her window had shrunk to just over four hours.

Four hours, three cottages. They were small. Hopefully the guests wouldn't have left them in too much of a state.

How did holiday guests leave cottages, anyway? Was it normal to clean up, or to leave the place the way her Cameron left his room on cleaning day?

She was about to find out.

It took an hour to get Cottage Two gleaming. She made mental notes as she went, aware that the other cottages would be identical. That made things easier, at least.

The cottages were all painted a neutral cream, with the same furniture and the same decorations.

As she went, she learned. The most efficient way to polish the dining table and rearrange the sofa cushions. How long the water in the kitchen took to get hot. The tricky shower screen, which she'd have no problem with in the other cottages after struggling with it the first time.

Even the artwork was the same. Rosamund ran a duster over the giant painting of a cream tea above the mantelpiece. She stood back and nodded. The scone in the picture was spread with jam first and then cream.

The Dorset way. The correct way, as far as Rosamund was concerned.

Just a mile or two away over the border in Devon, they would spread the cream and then the jam. But whoever had chosen this photograph knew their audience.

She left Cottage Two feeling optimistic; she was ahead.

But then came Cottage Three.

It was a disaster zone. Piles of unwashed crockery, two broken plates, vomit across one of the beds, and a suspicious smell of urine that took her a good twenty minutes to track down to the settee in the lounge.

She swallowed down bile. "Oh, my goodness!"

Sorting out the kitchen and cleaning up vomit were time sucks, but nothing compared to the mystery urine. How would she get rid of it?

She settled for soaking it with upholstery cleaner, scrubbing it with the used towels, then dragging the whole thing into the back yard to sit in the sunshine.

Rosamund checked her watch; a whole hour, lost. And it would never dry in time for the Marconis' scheduled arrival at three.

She stared at the cushions, thinking. She could tackle this.

Then it came to her. She smiled to herself, then opened up the unoccupied Cottage Five.

She hurried to Cottage Five, pausing for a car leaving Cottage Four. The Obengs, she presumed, out to enjoy the final day of their holiday. She glanced through the cottage's front window – it looked tidy, which boded well for tomorrow at least – and spotted that same picture she'd seen in the other cottages. The Dorset cream tea, jam first and then cream.

It took just five minutes to swap the sofa cushions from Five with the damp ones from Three. She could deal with those tomorrow.

Pulling in a deep breath, Rosamund sprinted to Cottage Six, bracing herself.

Please, not more mess.

The Dorset Cream Tea Mystery

But it was fine. And her learning had paid off; the whole cottage took thirty minutes.

As she left the cottage, its new occupants were arriving. She gave them a wave and drove away.

Did it.

Chapter Four

Rosamund filled in a report on her cleaning activities. Someone at head office would need to replenish those plates in the stock cupboard. Head office was Hewish Homes, owned by Annie's cousin Gillian. Annie wasn't fond of Gillian.

The Lyme Regis Women's Swimming Club had a WhatsApp group, and there was a message from Annie.

How was your first shift of housekeeping?

Rosamund had spent most of her life putting on a brave face and pretending everything was fine. But that hadn't worked in her favour so much, recently. And these were her friends.

Wasn't everything I hoped for, if I'm honest. One cottage was a real mess. I think next time I'll do a triage pass, check to see how I need to divide my time.

Yes. She'd do that.

Ah, so you learned something. That means it was a good day!

Rosamund smiled at Annie's positivity.

Thank you, you're so right!

When she recounted the experience the next day at the beach, the others had their own insights.

"Actual vomit?" Figgy whispered. "Vomit from other humans? They left it there? Urine too?"

Rosamund was starting to wish she hadn't mentioned it.

"God, Figgy! Have you met people?" Helen rolled her eyes. "There are some truly appalling specimens out there. We get them in the gallery. The ones that don't stop their kids smearing chocolate across the exhibits. Absolute monsters."

"I do like to imagine that most people are basically good," said Annie. "Although there's that quote, isn't there? About how ethical behaviour is doing the right thing when nobody's watching."

"Sounds about right," agreed Helen.

"I reckon some people imagine that when they close the door behind them on their messed-up holiday cottage, nobody will know it was them. Surely you can report people who leave it in a horrible state?"

"I don't know," said Rosamund. "I'll find out."

They trooped over to get their hot drinks from the kiosk, then spent a good half hour trying to guess what might lie in store for Rosamund next time, while Helen tested the limits of Figgy's disgust with increasingly outlandish suggestions for how bodily fluids might be presented.

"Of course," she said with an exaggerated shudder, "the one thing you should never do is get a blacklight and switch it on in any kind of hotel or rental room."

Figgy looked at her. "A what?"

"Blacklight," explained Annie. "Sort of like a UV torch. Makes things glow when other lights are out."

Figg's brow creased. "Things?"

"Bodily fluids."

"Urine," said Rosamund. "Blood traces. Any human *fluids*."

"It'll light up like a Christmas tree!" added Helen. "Tried it once in a hotel room. I ended up sleeping in the bath." She nodded. "True story."

"Why have you even got one of those blacklight things?" Annie asked. "We're talking about the kind of device the police use to find blood at a crime scene."

Helen shrugged. "I've got some at the gallery. We use them for displays sometimes. There are artists that like to work with the kind of inks and paints that fluoresce under a blacklight. Such fun."

Rosamund thought back to Cottage Three. She wrinkled her nose. "I don't think I'm inclined to borrow one."

Chapter Five

Dougie put the kettle on as he spotted DS Strunk pulling up in the car park outside Lyme Regis police station. The DS and a couple of colleagues from Headquarters had spent the whole of yesterday at the crime scene on Lyme Road.

The CSIs had recorded every detail before the body was taken off to Exeter for a post-mortem. DS Strunk's boss, DI Hannah Patterson, had pointed out that, what with Tarone being heavily involved in the Devon criminal fraternity, his death might become a Devon and Cornwall Police case. Her old patch, and, if the rumours were true, one she was still loyal to.

Douglas was already putting teabags in cups by the time the DS came through to the office.

"You can't stay away, can you?" he said, with a smile.

The DS rolled his eyes. "I actually enjoy getting out of HQ. And I appreciate the charm of spending time in Lyme, rather than the mean streets of Bournemouth."

Douglas snorted. Bournemouth came with its own issues, but it was hardly New York or the East End of London.

Over a cup of tea and ginger nut biscuit, the DS explained where they stood.

"Initial post-mortem is as we suspected. Tarone was stabbed in the gut and bled out. He wasn't stabbed at the scene – not enough blood – but he died there, more than a day ago. Weapon's nowhere in the vicinity."

"Nasty business," said Sergeant Connor, entering to collect his cuppa and handful of biscuits.

DS Strunk looked up at him. "There is an angle you all need to be aware of."

Douglas raised an eyebrow. The sarge sat down with a groan – he wasn't getting any younger.

The DS sipped his tea. "Seems there's something of a turf war going on in Devon. The Freeman Family are an offshoot of the Kelvins, who you might have heard of. Tarone worked for them."

Douglas frowned. "I thought they were all dead or in prison." Tina had mentioned the Kelvins enough times. Based out of Poole, they were a thoroughly nasty lot.

The DS shook his head. "Arthur Kelvin and his two nephews, yes. But George Freeman was a cousin. Or a sort of cousin. Close enough that Kyle Kelvin – one of those nephews – had no problem with him helping expand family operations into Devon a couple of years back. Anyway, now Kyle's in prison, the Freemans have been growing their operations. With Tarone at the centre of things."

"But he pissed the Freemans off, so they killed him?" Douglas suggested. "Overstepped, maybe."

The DS shook his head. "Not as simple as that. There's a newer gang, capitalising on the fact that the Freemans aren't as savvy as Kyle Kelvin was. The Shkozas. Another offshoot, this time of a London gang. The two gangs have had what you might call a bit of a spat over who controls the drug supply. Poor Anthony Tarone isn't the only recent victim."

"Other murders?" the sarge asked through a mouthful of biscuit.

DS Strunk's mouth twitched. "One of the Shkoza family is in intensive care with a gunshot injury. There was also an arson attack on a house in Torquay. No one died, thank God, but there's two people in hospital with smoke inhalation. It's all, as they say, kicking off."

"Too right it is," muttered the sarge, almost spitting out biscuit crumbs, then catching them in his hand.

DS Strunk looked at him and licked his lips. "But here's the thing," he said. "Tommy Freeman, notional head of the family since his dad George died last year – kidney failure, if you're wondering – he disappeared two days ago and hasn't been seen since."

Douglas had forgotten Wendy, sitting at her desk while this conversation was going on. He jumped as she pushed her chair back, then flushed.

"You think Tommy Freeman is on the run?" she asked. "You reckon he came this way?"

"It's a possibility," said the DS.

She pushed her chair closer. "He and Anthony Tarone were running from a Shkoza hit squad—"

The DS shared a look with the sarge. "Not exactly the language I would choose, constable."

Wendy leaned back. "Sorry. And Anthony gets stabbed and maybe Tommy is on the run in the countryside nearby."

"We don't know," said DS Strunk, nodding along

anyway. "We think you ought to be on the lookout for anything suspicious."

"Mysterious figures spotted in the woods," said Wendy.

Sergeant Connor grunted a laugh. "Sounds like we're looking for Big Foot now."

"I'm just asking you to keep your eyes open," said the DS.

"Oh, we can definitely do that," agreed Douglas.

Chapter Six

Rosamund was determined not to be wrong-footed on her next visit to the cottages. She looked at her list.

Saturday
Cottage 1 – Taverner leaving – Clean – Quinns arriving today
Cottage 2 – Occupied (Arrowsmiths)
Cottage 3 – Occupied (Marconis)
Cottage 4 – Obengs leaving – Clean – Hollandes arriving today
Cottage 5 – Unoccupied – Clean – Jones arriving today
Cottage 6 – Occupied (Drummonds)

She did her triage pass through the day's cottages, gathering laundry as she went.

Five had been empty for a week and would be easy – just some light dusting, cushion plumping and stocking the fridge with the welcome pack. And Four looked as straightforward as she'd been expecting from yesterday's glance through the window, so she entered Cottage One feeling more positive.

As she opened the door, she was surprised to see a woman standing in the living room.

"Can I help you?" said Rosamund.

The young woman had brown frizzy hair tied back in pigtails with two bobbles. In her arm was a caddy of cleaning supplies.

"Just finished cleaning," she said.

Rosamund pointed to the Hewish Holiday Homes logo on the apron she wore. "*I'm* the housekeeper."

"Oh," said the woman, smiling brightly. "So am I! We must be double booked."

The place did seem clean. There was a smell of cleaning products, quite an overpowering smell, in fact. The scent was unpleasantly floral and cloying, and Rosamund could imagine herself getting a headache if she breathed it in for much longer.

"I've not seen you before," she said. "Who are you?"

"Morgan." The pig-tailed woman was still smiling. "Cleaner. Very sorry to intrude. I'll be off now."

She went to the front door and let herself out.

Rosamund frowned, wondering what had just happened. Had she left the door unlocked yesterday? No. She was certain she'd locked it.

She heard a scraping noise from outside. The key safe.

Was the woman putting the key back?

Rosamund went outside, hearing the loud click of the safe closing. The woman was walking away.

"Ta-ra!" The mysterious Morgan turned to wave, then continued on her way.

Rosamund stood in the doorway, puzzled. It was possible

that the woman was another cleaner. But there was something about the interaction – and the unpleasantly powerful cleaning product smell – that set Rosamund's nerves jangling with suspicion.

She decided to call Eileen, the woman who organised the cleaners for the cottages.

"Morgan?" said Eileen. "Not got a Morgan on our books. Describe her."

Rosamund did.

"Nope," said Eileen. "Not ringing any bells."

"Maybe someone else booked her."

"No one sorts the cleaning but me," said Eileen. "Sure she wasn't the guest?"

"No," Rosamund replied. "The occupant was, um, Taverner. One man. A last-minute booking. And this woman had cleaning stuff. No suitcase or anything."

"And you didn't imagine this?"

Rosamund suppressed a growl and ended the call as quickly as possible.

Eileen might not have been bothered, but Rosamund couldn't let it go. She wanted to call the police, but what would they do? Clearly the woman knew the code for the key safe, and had let herself in. Perhaps she'd been a guest in the past. The code would need to be changed, it was as simple as that.

Still uncertain, she decided to message Annie. With a daughter and a son-in-law in the police force, she might have some insight.

Can I ask you something? she typed to Annie.

Sure thing, chickadee, came the almost instant reply. *Want to chat?*

A chat would be good; she was feeling quite shaken. Rosamund dialled Annie.

"What's up, hun?" Annie asked, picking up on the first ring.

"It's the cottages."

"Another one trashed?" Annie sounded vaguely amused.

Rosamund frowned. "No. Nothing like that. There was a woman. She let herself into one of the cottages while I was working."

"She work for the company?"

"She wasn't wearing a uniform. But she was standing there, in the living room, when I let myself in."

"She broke in?"

Rosamund swallowed. Was she overreacting? But the woman hadn't been wearing a uniform. "Maybe," she said.

Silence.

"Annie?" Rosamund said, her voice small.

"You should report this to the police," her friend said.

"But she got the key from the key safe. That's not breaking in, is it?" Rosamund was beginning to think she had overreacted. "I don't want to waste police time."

"Rosamund, you're not wasting anyone's time. Listen, how about I have a word with Tina?"

Rosamund sighed. That sounded like a good compromise. "Thank you. She might know what to do for the best."

"Not a problem, chick. Now have you got more cleaning to do?"

Housekeeping, Rosamund thought, but didn't correct her. "Yes. Thanks Annie, I appreciate your support."

"No problem. It'll all be fine, don't you worry."

Chapter Seven

Rosamund certainly couldn't fault the mysterious Morgan's cleaning abilities. Downstairs was sparkling, even if she had overdone it with the air fresheners. It seemed she hadn't got to the upstairs before Rosamund's arrival, though.

Rosamund hoovered upstairs, cleaned the bathroom, and left the windows open while she moved on to Cottage Four.

As she'd noted in her triage pass, the Obengs hadn't left her any challenges. She changed the beds, dusted and then came downstairs.

All of the cottages had a large kitchen that led onto a communal seating area. It was a convivial space, and Rosamund imagined it filled with family groups staying in the cottages.

The bookcase in the living room, which she always dusted, held cookery books, reference books about fossils, and some coffee table books showcasing Dorset at its best. Plenty of inspiration for a holiday in Lyme Regis.

Above the mantelpiece on the cream-coloured wall was

that same picture of the cream tea, the one she'd spotted through the window yesterday. Rosamund hadn't eaten a full cream tea in ages, but if she was exposed to this picture every morning...

She sprayed the table and wiped it with her damp cloth. As she did so, something clicked in her mind.

She looked up at the cream tea photograph again. It had the cream first, and then the jam.

Impossible.

It was a different picture to those in the other cottages. It was broadly similar, a sort of impressionistic painting of a cream tea in summer's golden light. But this cream tea was being eaten in the Devon way.

"What the hell?"

She put down the cloth and the spray bottle. Her hands went to her hips as she stared at the picture.

Rosamund wasn't a daydreamer. She knew her own mind, and she knew she wasn't imagining things. What on earth was going on?

She pulled out her phone and took a picture, then got back to the cleaning. There was no time to stand still pondering.

She worked her way through the cottages systematically, her mind working through the two peculiar things she'd encountered.

The uninvited woman in Cottage One, and then the picture. She'd seen it yesterday, she was sure of it. It had very definitely changed in Cottage Four.

When she reached Cottage Five, she went straight to the picture.

There it was, in the Dorset tradition. Jam and then

cream. She took a photo and flicked back and forth between the two images on her phone.

"This makes no sense."

Rosamund dropped the two photos into the WhatsApp group to share with the Lyme Regis Women's Swimming Club.

Check these out. Each of these cottages has the same picture showing a Dorset cream tea. The picture in Cottage Four has been changed since yesterday to show a Devon one. What do we make of that?

Helen was the first to answer. *Heathens!*

Rosamund laughed. It felt a bit less weird, now she was sharing it with her friends.

We stock prints of the Devon one in the gallery. Trite but commercial stuff. Sold one just the other day.

Annie sent a suggestion.

Maybe the next guest is from Devon? Someone there is keen to impress!

"Huh," Rosamund said to herself.

Who would have time to do such a thing? As far as Rosamund knew, she was the only person who went into the cottages between guests. She looked at the list of upcoming guests to see if there was any additional detail given.

Cottage Four was going to be home to the Hollande family, from Wales.

Rosamund messaged Annie back.

Next family are from Wales.

Bloody mystery then, isn't it? replied Annie.

Chapter Eight

Rosamund had just moved on to Cottage Five when there was a knock at the door.

She went downstairs to open it.

"Tina! How lovely to see you."

Annie's daughter was still on maternity leave from her job in Dorset CID or whatever name her department had. She had been in Lyme Regis for several weeks now, on account of her husband Mike, a fellow detective, having accidentally trashed their house with some failed DIY.

"You didn't have to make a special trip."

Tina shrugged. "Nice to get out of the house."

"The family well?"

Tina nodded. "Mum's got the kids. Mike's dad is threatening to visit, which is causing a headache."

Rosamund frowned. "I thought the two of them were... estranged."

"Very much so. But Dante Legg, very much out of character, has decided he would like to get to know his grandchildren. Madness really. How can people obsess over their grandchildren when they barely speak to their own kids?"

Rosamund smiled. "Tell me about it. My mum spoils Cameron rotten from afar. I'm not sure the two of us could tolerate each other if she was any closer."

Tina nodded. "So, what's the funny business here then?"

Rosamund ushered her inside. "Honestly, Tina, I just wanted to get some advice from you."

Tina stepped over the threshold in that way police officers did. Rosamund thought it was mildly impolite but stepped aside anyway.

"Mum says there's been a break in." Tina stood in the kitchen, looking round.

Tina had tracked footprints across the damp floor. Rosamund would need to go back over that with the mop before she left.

"Not this place," she said. "Cottage One. Listen, do you mind if I work while we talk? Time's so tight on the turnaround."

"Right." Tina went to sit on the sofa, but stopped, spotting the cushions stacked up on end.

"Oh." Rosamund gestured at the cushions. "The guests from Cottage Three left something unspeakable on the sofa. I had to clean them and swapped them with the cushions here while they dried."

"Wow. So, tell me what's gone on."

Rosamund had already sprayed the cooker, so now she tackled the grease stains as she talked. "The first thing to know is that these six cottages are identical down to the last teaspoon. It must make life easier when it comes to getting spares. Hewish owns them."

"Ah yes. My great-aunt Gillian."

"I don't deal directly with Gillian. There's a woman called Eileen who organises the cleaning."

Rosamund watched as Tina wrote details into her notebook.

"And you clean just these six? Or are there others?"

"Oh, Hewish Homes has loads of cottages. I only just started, so I'm doing these six," Rosamund told her. "I think they want to see how I get on, which is why I don't want to make a fuss."

Tina gave her a look. "You need to make a fuss if someone's gaining unauthorised entry. That's not safe for guests."

"True."

"Talk me through what happened this morning."

"I did a triage pass on all the cottages I was due to clean. A quick look to see if there were any with big clean-up problems. I worked my way down – Five, Four, One — and when I went into Cottage One there was this woman there."

"Could you have left the door unlocked from another time?"

Rosamund turned to give her a look. "Definitely not."

"Is there any chance she could have been the previous guest, just late leaving the property?"

"No. I have a list. Taverner, a single man, was the last guest. The woman said her name was Morgan."

"First name or last name?"

Good question. "No idea."

Tina nodded. "Well, it goes without saying that the key safe can't be considered secure. You need to talk to Eileen about getting a new code."

"Yes. I'll do that."

Rosamund wasn't sure whether to tell Tina about the other part. It sounded so trivial and unlikely.

"Listen, there's another thing. It's a bit peculiar really."

"Go on."

Rosamund pointed at the photo. Tina sat at the table, close to where it hung. "That photo of a cream tea."

Tina smiled. "Dorset cream tea. Jam first."

"Yes!" Rosamund smiled. "All of them have the same picture. I'm certain." She pulled out her phone and found the picture from Cottage Four. "See this?"

Tina peered at the image. "Huh. Cream first."

"Exactly. It's different in Cottage Four. I'm wondering if someone switched it."

"Or perhaps they were always different?"

"No." Rosamund shook her head. "I looked through the window yesterday. I am certain that the picture has been changed."

"Hm."

Tina stood up. "Well, magically transformed pictures are perhaps a bit beyond me. But I think it's time you let me take a look at Cottage One, don't you?"

Together, the two of them poked around Cottage One. The open windows had cleared much of the over powering smell, but Rosamund's unease lingered.

"Nothing stolen?" Tina suggested to Rosamund.

"What is there to take?" said Rosamund. "TV, microwave, coffee maker. They're all here. Unless she was looking for something the last guest left behind."

Tina shrugged. "I guess you could contact the previous occupant. Taverner, you say? I assume you have contact details."

"The company will have," Rosamund replied. "I could ask them."

Tina's smile was uncertain. "And yet, nothing seems wrong. Nothing out of place."

Rosamund sighed.

Tina pointed at the picture over the mantelpiece. "And at least this one has the right picture."

Chapter Nine

The discovery of a second body near Lyme Regis in the space of a week was, in Douglas's opinion, an unnecessary coincidence.

The police had been called out to a piece of farmland off the main road two miles west of the town. The initial call had been in the early light of dawn, when smoke was spotted over the derelict tractor sheds.

Douglas had attended expecting to find an accidental fire or an act of vandalism. Instead, he'd found a carefully constructed fire with a human body at its centre. The stink of smoke and petrol hung over the scene.

He'd held his nose until back-up arrived. At this rate, they'd need to order more crime scene tape.

DS Strunk was there within the hour, yawning as he got out of his car.

"Mornings." He nodded at Douglas. "Not sure I can cope with them."

Douglas grunted. "We've got Tina's newborn at home, remember? I swear we're all operating on low battery power."

"Tina enjoying maternity leave?" the DS asked.

"Itching to get back, more like. Yesterday she was out at some holiday cottages, helping one of her mum's friends investigate a mysterious cleaning."

"Mysterious cleaning?"

"Yup." Douglas smiled. "A woman broke in and cleaned one of the cottages."

The DS laughed. "That's the kind of crime I'd like to investigate." He pointed to the still-smouldering fire. "Let's take a look."

Douglas gave him an overview as they walked over.

"Dead body, brought out here to be disposed of," said DS Strunk. "A man, by the look of it."

"I think so."

The DS stroked his chin. "You know what would be a convenient explanation?"

"What?"

"That this is Tommy Freeman. Him and his man, Anthony Tarone, on the run from the vengeful Shkoza gang, make it out here. Tarone bled out by the side of the road, but Tommy managed to hide a little longer before the Shkozas caught up with him. And here we are."

"Convenient?" said Douglas. "It means there's still a killer out there."

"But only one killer, or at least one set of killers. Better if this is all connected rather than having two random acts of violence in your charming sleepy town."

Douglas eyed him. "Don't reckon you can call this place sleepy now, can you?"

Chapter Ten

Sunday morning. Rosamund's swim would normally clear her head. But it wasn't working.

With the possible exception of Juniper, a young athletic Australian, Rosamund was usually out there longer than anyone else, but today she wasn't feeling the sea's magic touch. She headed back to shore.

As she walked back up the beach with Figgy, skin goose-bumped from the cold sea, Figgy turned to her and said, "You've got wrinkles in your forehead."

"I've what?"

"I don't mean old lady wrinkles. I mean you look worried."

"Oh." Rosamund attempted to unfurrow her brow. "It's this strange business at the cottages. I just can't shake it."

"You've really taken it to heart," Figgy said.

"I don't like things that don't make sense."

There was a squawk. Up on the sea wall where the swimmers left their belongings, two seagulls were arguing over a scrap of food. As they danced back and forth over the various items, a towel came loose and dropped to the sand.

"Kevin!" Figgy ran forward, shooing the pair away.

Rosamund gave her a look. "Did you recognise that seagull?"

"Of course."

"I wondered if you called all seagulls Kevin."

Figgy frowned. "That would be very strange behaviour."

"Well, yes..."

Figgy picked up the towel and placed it back on the bags lined up on the wall.

"So, why don't you tell me all about your cottage cleaning problem," she said.

Rosamund detected a note of condescension. Figgy, who had been a virtual recluse for many months, was working on her social skills. They still needed some polishing.

"I'm sure I've explained the matter already," she said.

"True, but I'm not sure I fully understood."

And so, while they dried off, Rosamund went over it again. The changed picture in Cottage Four, the woman who had broken in and inexplicably cleaned Cottage One.

"I'm sure I've got a headache from the horrible air freshener she used in there," added Rosamund.

"Two mysteries in one day," said Figgy, as Helen and Annie came up to the sea wall to dry off.

"Two mysteries?" asked Annie.

"The intruder and the changed picture."

"Ah."

"This isn't my towel," said Helen, picking up the towel the seagull had knocked to the ground.

Annie took it from her.

"It fell," said Figgy. "I thought it belonged there."

Annie flapped it out then towelled herself down. "Tina came round and had a look at the cottages though, didn't she?"

"Very kind of her," said Rosamund.

Helen snorted. "I should imagine the police have more important things to do."

"Not officially on the force at the moment, as you well know," said Annie. "But yes. I heard from Naomi's Dougie—"

"Overheard, more like," put in Helen.

"That there's been another body found, this one by Hatchett's farm."

Rosamund put a hand to her chest. "Another stabbing?"

"They think this chap's been shot."

"Dreadful," muttered Figgy.

Helen wrapped her dry-robe around herself and slipped on a pair of kitsch fifties sunglasses. The sun was already hot.

"This business with the changed picture," she said. "There is one simple explanation."

"Is there?" asked Rosamund.

"You were saying that some people had left their cottage in a terrible state."

"The Tyne-Phillips. Cottage Three. Disgusting, you may recall me saying."

"And the people who were in the cottage with the changed picture...?"

"Cottage Four. The, um, Obengs, it was."

"Did they leave their cottage in a state?"

"Not at all. Tidied up after themselves."

"There you go," said Helen. "I find there are two types of people in this world."

"Yes?"

"One the one hand, there are the loose cannons and children of nature who create merry chaos in the world as they dance through it. Like Annie here."

"I'm like what?" said Annie, who had been towelling her hair and not listening.

"A child of nature," said Figgy, bringing a smile to Annie's lips.

"A loose cannon," added Helen, which tempered the smile. "And then there are the prudish and repressed neat freaks who tidy up after themselves and put the pieces back together."

Helen was looking at Rosamund.

Rosamund pointed to herself. "Am I...?"

"Oh, goodness me, yes," Helen said. "And it sounds like those people in Cottage Four might have been the same. Left the place neat and tidy. But what if they broke the picture in the cottage by accident? What would a neat freak do?"

"Tell someone," suggested Figgy.

Rosamund shook her head. Helen was right. "They'd try to replace it."

Annie clicked her fingers. "Didn't you say in the chat that you sold one of those prints in your gallery the other day?"

"My thought exactly," said Helen, with an arched eyebrow.

"That... that could actually work," Rosamund said. "Do you remember who bought the print?"

"Just about. It was a woman. What did the neat freak look like?"

"The Obengs. I saw them go out in their car. The mother had a shaved head. Quite striking."

"Ah," said Helen. "Not her, then. This woman definitely had hair. Long and frizzy. In two bunches, almost pigtails."

Rosamund gasped. "Pigtails? But that's the woman who broke in."

"This just gets stranger," said Annie.

"Actually, no," said Figgy, thoughtfully.

"No?" asked Helen and Rosamund as one.

A slow smile crept over Figgy's face. "It's like the towels here."

"Pardon?" said Helen.

"The towel Kevin knocked off. There was an accident. The towel gets put back. But we put it with the wrong bag. It's... it's like the sofa you cleaned!" Figgy grinned. "Cottage Three messed up the sofa, yes?"

"Piddled all over it," said Annie.

"Yes, but in cleaning it up, Rosamund swapped the cushions with the ones in another cottage."

"I did," said Rosamund. "Are these things linked?"

"Only as an example. What if it was Cottage One where things got trashed, including the picture?"

"But it was neat and tidy when I got there."

"Because this Morgan the cleaner had been in. She replaced the broken picture with the one from Cottage Four and then tidied up."

Rosamund frowned. This made no sense. "Why would she move a picture if she was going to buy a replacement?"

Annie grunted. "She'd already bought the replacement and realised it didn't quite match. She thought someone else might notice, too, and she was right. So she swapped them, just like you swapped the cushions. She didn't want anyone to notice she'd tidied up in Cottage One."

"That seems like a lot of effort to go to."

"You know what?" said Annie, gathering her things. "I think it's about time all of us had a look at this mysterious cottage."

Rosamund looked at her. "What? Now?"

"But what about our morning coffees and hot chocolates?" complained Figgy.

Annie flashed her eyes at the younger woman. "We'll get them to go!"

Chapter Eleven

Rosamund felt peculiar turning up at her place of work with three friends in tow, especially since two of them were dressed in swimming costumes and dry robes and swigging takeout coffees. But here they were, at Clappentail Cottages.

"Is it this one?" Annie marched up to Cottage One.

"Just wait a minute." Rosamund got out her notebook to check what she was certain she already knew. "Sunday. It's occupied. The Quinn family are staying here."

"They won't mind some visitors, will they?"

"This feels awkward." Figgy shifted from foot to foot.

"Relish the awkward." Helen took hold of her elbow.

Rosamund braced herself and knocked on the door. She waited a minute and knocked again. There was no response.

"They might have gone out."

"Good." Annie was already standing by the keysafe. "You can let us in, then."

Rosamund didn't really want to get fired so soon after starting her job. But she squashed down those feelings, retrieved the key from the combination keysafe and opened the door.

She peered inside. "Here we are. Touch nothing."

They entered together. The cottage was tidy but for a hoodie tossed over the back of a chair and two empty cereal bowls on the coffee table.

"The mystery cleaning woman was here, then?" asked Figgy.

Annie wrinkled her nose. "I see what you mean about the smell."

Annie was right. The smell was still in the air, even after a day. Although it had changed. And now it had changed, Rosamund thought...

"That's not cleaning product," said Helen, sniffing mightily. "That's paint."

She was right.

The smell hanging in the air was definitely the remnants of fresh paint.

"That woman did some painting, too?" said Annie. "Blimey, she's a busy bee."

"I didn't even notice," said Rosamund. "Because of the overwhelming perfume smell."

Figgy gestured around them. "Used to mask the smell of paint."

Rosamund still wasn't convinced. "This is making less and less sense. There was a broken picture, so she swapped it for the one in Cottage Four and then replaced that with one from Helen's shop. And then she painted and cleaned the place."

"Maybe they made even more mess, and she had to cover it up," suggested Figgy.

"But this business with swapping the paintings..."

"Except," interjected Annie. "Let's say they made a really big mess in here and had to replace the picture."

"We know that."

"But this cleaner woman, Morgan, couldn't find an exact match. She found a picture with a Devon cream tea – cream then jam – not a Dorset one – jam then cream. The wrong picture would draw your eye, as it did. But she didn't want you looking at the picture in here."

"Whyever not?" asked Rosamund.

Annie approached the picture on the wall and reached out to take hold of it.

Figgy stepped forward. "I thought we weren't touching anything."

Rosamund said nothing. She watched as Annie took the painting off the wall. There was nothing behind it.

No, wait. There was a hole. Cracks in the plaster, and then a hole through to the brickwork about the diameter of a one pence coin.

Annie spoke in a quiet voice. "Is it me or does that look like a bullet hole?"

Figgy gasped. "Oh, my."

"I've got to go get something from the shop." Helen dashed out. "Touch nothing!"

Rosamund approached to inspect the hole more closely. It did indeed look like a bullet hole.

"Annie," she said, "I think you'd better call one of the police officers in your family, don't you think?"

Chapter Twelve

There was no distinction between week and weekend for coppers on shift work. Sunday was rarely a day of rest. But Douglas always tried to generate a Sunday feeling at work.

This meant putting classical music on the radio and opening a fresh packet of biscuits. He liked to think it created a peaceful, even contemplative air.

At least, for as long as the peace lasted.

"Damn it all!" DS Strunk slid his phone into his pocket as he entered the office.

"Good morning, DS Strunk?" Douglas offered him the first biscuit in the freshly opened pack.

The DS ignored the biscuits. "No. Not really. Possibly. Not sure."

Douglas looked at him for an explanation.

"Post-mortem is finished on the body in the fire," said DS Strunk.

"Tommy Freeman?"

"*Not* Tommy Freeman. Fingerprints show it to be one Aleksander Goga."

The name meant nothing to Douglas.

"Enforcer for the Shkosa family," the DS added.

"Ah. So one body from the Freeman crime gang and one from the Shkosas. The first stabbed, the second shot."

A nod. "Bullet went clean through. Post-mortem says he was shot elsewhere and then taken to the farm to be disposed of."

"So we're still looking for Tommy Freeman?"

Another nod. "Current theory – my theory – is that Tommy and Anthony Tarone were fleeing this way, knowing the Skhosas were hot on their heels. Tarone had a stab injury, maybe from whatever went down in Exeter. Tommy left him to bleed out on the side of the road and then hid out elsewhere."

"And then this Goga character catches up with Tommy."

"Right. But Tommy's got a gun. We know the Freemans have used them on occasion."

"Tommy shoots Goga and disposes of him, and, what, it's possible he's still in the area?"

"Depends on whether he thinks it's too dangerous to move on or too dangerous to stay."

Douglas's phone was ringing. Tina.

"We printed off Tommy's mugshot," he said. "We can go asking around. 'Scuse me."

He picked up the phone.

"Morning."

"Hey, Dougie," said Tina. "Are you still looking for someone in connection with that gunshot victim the other day?"

"We were just talking about it."

"We?"

"Me and DS Strunk."

"I think you both need to come over to Clappentail Cottages."

"Off Silver Street?"

"Yep. My mum and her friends have just found something you might want to look at."

Chapter Thirteen

Cottage One was getting crowded.

Helen had dashed off and now Tina had turned up, dressed like a new mother forced to leave the house early on a Sunday morning. She'd taken a look at the hole in the wall and murmured several things to herself before calling her brother-in-law at the station.

Then the Quinn family had arrived, all five of them, freshly returned from a morning walk on the beach and breakfast at Breaststrokes café-bar. They had questions about why there were four women standing around in their living room.

Both Tina (as representative of law and order) and Rosamund (as representative of the letting company) tried to explain. The Quinns, to their credit, found the whole thing fascinating and peculiar rather than annoying.

Tina tapped Rosamund's arm.

"The people who rented this place, the day before this was found..."

"Taverner." Rosamund got out her notebook to check. "One man. Taverner. A last minute booking."

"And how would he have booked?"

"We'd have to ask Eileen. She organises things."

Five minutes later, Tina was on the phone to Eileen and noting down the debit card details as they were read out to her.

Helen burst through the door, her face red from running.

"Got it!"

"Got what?" asked Annie.

"Got what?" shouted the youngest of the Quinn family, who was enjoying the spectacle.

Helen waggled a slim torch. "Blacklight."

"Oh, for spotting pee stains," said Figgy.

"And more besides!" Helen grinned. "Quick. Let's close the curtains. Get the doors."

Rosamund nipped upstairs to close the bedroom doors and the curtains on the half-stair. Annie had closed the door to the kitchen and was tugging at the living room curtains when Tina, now on the phone to her colleagues, asked, "What are you doing? This might be a crime scene."

Helen ignored Tina and went to close the front door, where the Quinns were crowded.

"In or out?"

The Quinn family, taken with the little drama, stepped inside. There were now nine people in the almost entirely dark living room.

"This is no way to preserve a crime scene," said Tina.

"Good job you're not a proper copper at the moment, then," replied her mum.

Helen flicked on the blacklight torch. A pale blue glow

washed over the room and the Quinn children, as well as Figgy, gasped.

As it passed over different objects, the level of light reflected changed. Rosamund wondered if flashes of bright light would show up spots that previous cleaners had failed to clean, spelling out their own little horror story.

Helen played the light over the cream-coloured walls and the mantelpiece.

Rosamund had expected bright splats of reflected light to reveal some horrific evidence. There were no bright marks, but there was an uneven tone to the paint under the UV light. Streaks of light and dots of dark.

"I thought things glowed under blacklight," said Figgy.

"Urine does," said Tina, stepping forward. Her hand hovered over the darker ovals and dots on the wall. "But blood soaks up UV light."

"Blood?" squeaked one of the Quinn children, thrilled rather than fearful.

"But the wall's been painted," said Rosamund.

Tina nodded. "One coat, maybe."

She stared at it for a long moment, then said, "Right. Everyone out now. This is definitely a crime scene."

Everyone trooped outside into the daylight.

"I think we might want to stay somewhere else," Mrs Quinn said to Rosamund in a polite but firm tone.

"I understand."

"I think we'll be taking another trip to the beach and will expect to be moved on our return."

"I'll see what I can do. Take your time. There's some lovely fossil hunting towards Charmouth."

There was the sound of engines, and as a police car pulled into the yard, those occupants of the other cottages who had not yet come out to see the commotion also emerged. Douglas Anderson strode over to chat to Tina, giving a nod to the swimming ladies as he passed.

"I need a sit down and a stiff drink," Helen said to the others. "But in the absence of a stiff drink, I think I'll just have a sit down."

There was a bench opposite the cottages. The four women just about managed to squeeze onto it, side by side.

"So that was a murder scene," said Figgy.

"Seems it," said Rosamund. "I guess the woman I met was indeed actually a cleaner. In the criminal sense."

"A hitman!" Figgy cried. "I mean, a hitwoman!"

"OK, not in that sense. I meant a crime scene cleaner, in this case one who cleans up to hide the fact a crime has been committed there."

"Are there such people?"

"Oh, yes," said Annie. "I watched a whole series about it on Netflix. Very good stuff."

Helen looked at Rosamund. "Her job was to hide the fact that someone had been killed there. The fatal bullet went through the picture into the wall."

"I bet if the police retrieve that they could match it to the gun that fired it," said Annie.

Rosamund thought back to the mystery woman. "Our cleaner didn't want anyone to find it," she said. "That's why the woman put the odd-one-out picture in a different cottage. If I hadn't actually met her there in Cottage One, we'd never have thought about that place at all."

"She swapped the picture of the cream teas over," added Annie. "Then where there were bloody red marks on the wall which she couldn't wipe off, she got a matching cream paint and covered them up."

"Jam then cream," mused Helen. "The Dorset way."

"Oh, bad taste," Figgy pulled a face.

"Quite droll," said Annie.

Douglas sauntered over to the bench, gripping his police vest with both hands in that way police officers did.

"Whenever there's some strange business going on in town, why do I find you lot in the thick of it?" he asked.

"Us lot?" said Helen. "That's the thanks we get for solving this mystery."

"Did we solve a mystery?" asked Annie.

"This is a vital piece of the puzzle," Douglas told her. "And I think I can tell you the card used to pay for this place was also used to pay for a room at a pub in town yesterday. And that a man, one Tommy Freeman, has now been taken into custody." He raised an eyebrow. "Right in the middle of his full English breakfast."

"The shooter?" said Figgy excitedly.

Douglas made a calming hand gesture.

"And what about the cleaner?" asked Rosamund.

"The cleaner?" he said. "Oh. Yes. I hope we'll catch up with her at some point."

A thought occurred to Rosamund. "Helen, when the woman came into your shop to buy the print, I assume she wasn't wearing gloves."

"I don't think so," said Helen.

Rosamund gave Douglas a look. "If this woman has a criminal record, you might find her fingerprints on the picture she bought, which is now above the mantelpiece in Cottage Four."

"Is that so?"

Douglas gave her a sharp nod of thanks and hurried off towards Cottage Four.

Annie took the lid off her take-out coffee and peered inside as though hoping to find more at the bottom.

"Well, Rosamund, I never knew that being a cleaner could be quite so exciting."

Rosamund cleared her throat. "Housekeeper, Annie, if you would. I prefer the term housekeeper."

* * *

Thank you for reading *The Dorset Cream Tea Mystery*. You can read more about the adventures of Annie and her swimming friends, Rosamund, Helen and Figgy, in the second book in the series, *A Brush with Death*.

Happy Reading
Rachel & Mille

Buy from book retailers or via the Rachel McLean website.

Also by Rachel McLean

The DI Zoe Finch Series – buy from book retailers or via the Rachel McLean website.

Deadly Wishes

Deadly Choices

Deadly Desires

Deadly Terror

Deadly Reprisal

Deadly Fallout

Deadly Christmas

Deadly Origins, the FREE Zoe Finch prequel

The Dorset Crime Series – buy from book retailers or via the Rachel McLean website.

The Corfe Castle Murders

The Clifftop Murders

The Island Murders

The Monument Murders

The Millionaire Murders

The Fossil Beach Murders

The Blue Pool Murders

The Lighthouse Murders

The Ghost Village Murders

The Poole Harbour Murders

The Chesil Beach Murders

...and more to come

The McBride & Tanner Series – buy from book retailers or via the Rachel McLean website.

Blood and Money

Death and Poetry

Power and Treachery

Secrets and History

The Cumbria Crime Series by Rachel McLean and Joel Hames – buy from book retailers or via the Rachel McLean website.

The Harbour

The Mine

The Cairn

The Barn

The Lake

The Wood

The Port

...and more to come

Also by Millie Ravensworth

The Cozy Craft Mysteries – Buy now in ebook and paperback

The Wonderland Murders

The Painted Lobster Murders

The Sequinned Cape Murders

The Swan Dress Murders

The Tie-Dyed Kaftan Murders

The Scarecrow Murders